Charco
and
The Christmas Foal

Published by Green Dragon Publishing
PO Box 375, Lymington SO41 1AQ

Text copyright © Mel Newman 2009
Illustrations copyright © Jo Mooring-Aldridge 2009

The rights of Mel Newman to be identified as the author and Jo
Mooring-Aldridge as the illustrator of this work have been asserted.

Green Dragon Publishing is a small business specialising in the
publication of fiction linked to ecology, the natural world and our
relationship with the creatures who share it.

Printed in Totton, Hampshire by Hobbs the Printers Limited

This is a work of fiction. Names, characters, places and incidents are
either the product of the author's imagination or, if real, are used
fictitiously.

3 5 7 9 10 8 6 4

A catalogue record for this book is available from the British Library
ISBN: 978-0-9563945-1-4

FSC
Mixed Sources
Product group from well-managed
forests and other controlled sources
Cert no. SA-COC-001530
www.fsc.org
© 1996 Forest Stewardship Council

Charcoal
and
The Christmas Foal

A Tale of the New Forest

Mel Newman

Illustrations by Jo Mooring Aldridge

www.greendragonpublishing.co.uk

With special thanks to:
June Coutts for permission to use her brand in a fictional context, Sue and Sally in the Verderers' office for their practical advice, Ness Harbour and Steve Reneaux for encouragement and editing, and to Alison Kennedy for sharing her wisdom.

To Morse, Jo-Jo
and the creatures of the New Forest.

Autumn

*I*t was a night of bats and badgers. As soon as Tess and Charcoal left the cottage they could hear furtive snuffling in the birchwood copse. Small dark shapes flitted through the air, swooping and gliding above their heads. Through  the branches of the yew tree, the moon shone pale and silver.

The wind blew in from the south west, bringing smells of sea spray, salt and gales. Between the gusts, the air was rich with peat bog, heather and dying bracken.

Charcoal gambolled ahead as they walked up the hill to a small stand of oak and holly. Looking out across the ragged moor, he heard the first low roar of a red stag in rut. The sound sent a ripple of excitement through his body from his paws to his tail. A new season had begun.

Autumn had come to the Forest.

In the shelter of the woods, Charcoal's nose was suddenly full of soft scents of fungi, clay and last year's leaves. Acorns cracked beneath Tess's feet. Beech nuts lay littered by the quickening gale.

Already the trees were a blaze of russet, red and amber. Leaves whirled on the wind and covered the forest floor. The river was coloured with their dancing shapes.

Heavy rain had fed the river until it had become swollen like a snake and burst its banks. The path was flooded but Tess and Charcoal clambered along the edge where tree roots made strong footholds.

"Careful Charkie!" called Tess as Charcoal leapt into the dark swirls of racing water.

The river caught hold of Charcoal and clutched him in its cold, wet grip. He snatched a fallen branch and tried to swim back with it. The current was too fierce. Struggling was useless. Instead he turned and swam with the flow but he refused to let go of the branch.

He let the river carry him until he reached a long, slow bend. Here the water was shallow and the current ran less quickly. With the fallen branch still clenched in his teeth, Charcoal scrambled up onto the bank. He placed the branch under a tree and shook happily, spraying water in every direction. Then he dived back in.

This time he rescued a flip-flop, which he dropped triumphantly at Tess's feet. Water streamed off his jet black coat.

"Thanks Charkie!" said Tess, laughing.

Charcoal waited to see where they were going next. They often walked in the Forest at night. Tess would spend ages watching the creatures that lived there. Charcoal knew how to stay still and quiet so as not to frighten them away. Chasing deer, birds or rabbits was just not his style and they seemed to know it.

He had lived in the New Forest with Tess for almost all of his life. The woods, the heaths, the streams and even the weather had become as much a part of him as he was part of them.

Charcoal stopped abruptly and listened. Through the ground under his paws, he could feel the thudding of hooves. Out on the moor, ponies were galloping up and down, calling to each other.

"Wind's got under their tails" said Tess. "Perhaps it's because of the storm coming."

Somehow, Charcoal didn't think so. He stood watching through the line of birch trees at the edge of the moor. He could smell panic.

A single high-pitched whinny came out of the distance. A stranger, thought Charcoal. That's what the other ponies were so excited about. It was in trouble.

He looked up at Tess. She often understood what he was thinking.

"Okay Charkie. Go on, lead the way." she said.

Charcoal led Tess across the open moor to the far side. From there he picked one of the pony paths, threading his way through the prickly gorse bushes.

Gradually, gorse and heather gave way to low cotton grass and bog myrtle. The smell of fear was getting stronger, mingled with the deep, dark scent of the valley mire. The strange pony's calls were becoming weaker, less hopeful.

Every few minutes, Charcoal looked back to make sure Tess was following. Darkness had filled the valley and the moon was trapped behind the rain clouds. Charcoal knew that Tess's eyes were not as good as  his. She was stumbling over mounds of sedge and moss. He slowed down so that she could see him and use his strong back to steady her on the slopes.

They were close now. Charcoal sensed that even Tess could smell the pony's body, warm and pungent in the night air. He paused, his nose twitching and his ears full of the sound of reeds thrashing in the wind. Tess walked on, calling him softly.

Suddenly the ground moved like liquid beneath them.

"Oh no!" said Tess. "We're in the mire."

The thin layer of sphagnum moss squelched like a wet sponge under their feet. Charcoal leapt back onto the path but Tess sank up to her ankles. To his relief, she grabbed his collar and pulled herself up after him before she sank any deeper.

From near where they had been standing Charcoal heard a short "huff". He knew that sound. It was the sound a pony makes when it wants you to know it is there but doesn't know who you are. He pointed his nose in the direction of the noise and narrowed his eyes. As if by magic, the clouds parted and the moon shone through.

There it was - a grey pony! It was well over its hocks in stinking mud. Every time it struggled, it seemed to sink a little deeper. There was something else about this pony. She was heavily in foal.

"Okay girl," said Tess, "It's okay." She breathed out slowly, keeping her heartbeat steady and calm. "How did you go and get stuck in there then?"

Silently, she took Charcoal's lead out of her pocket. It was a long piece of blue and white rope. She knotted one end to make a fixed loop. Then she threw it towards the pony's neck. The pony snorted and lunged away.

"Hey little girl" cooed Tess "wrong way."

This time the pony tried to move towards them but she seemed exhausted. Charcoal lay down on the path. He kept as still as he could, feeling the pony's despair in his bones.

A second throw and the rope fell around the frightened mare's neck. Tess pulled. The mare strained against her. For a moment it seemed as if she would pull Tess into the mire.

Charcoal stood up and whined. Tess could never pull the pony free. She wasn't strong enough.

Tess reached into her pocket and took out a mobile phone.

It wasn't long before headlights appeared and the Agister's Land Rover bumped along the path.

"Hmm. Doesn't look too bad." he said. "I don't think we need to call the rescue service out tonight."

He pulled a piece of board, a halter and a long stick out of the back of his car. He laid the board down on the mud and crawled across it to the pony. Then he passed the halter over her head and poked the long stick deep into the mud several times until he found what he was looking for.

"Thought so – not so deep here. Come on old girl, this way."

With a strong heave on the rope and plenty of encouragement, the Agister led her out of the mire.

"Looks like she could do with a good feed." said the Agister. "She's a pretty one though." He eased the halter off, leaving his hand on her mane.

"Do you know who she belongs to?" asked Tess. It was too dark to see if she had an owner's brand or if her tail had been cut in the special pattern to show she'd been counted in the drift and the commoner's fee paid.

"Let's have a look." said the Agister, pushing her gently towards the light.

Until that moment, the mare had remained still, her breathing heavy. Without any warning she took off: galloping into the night.

"Nothing much wrong with her legs then!" said the
Agister, "Looks like we'll have to wait to find out any more!"

Christmas

*T*he moon had waxed to full and waned to dark twice more before Tess and Charcoal saw the dapple grey mare again.

It was Christmas Eve. Charcoal was dozing by the wood-burning stove when Tess sighed and put down the piece of oak wood she had been carving into the shape of a kingfisher.

"Come on Charkie," she said, "I don't know about you but I need a walk!"

They set out under a thickening sky towards the place where the stream cut the wide moor. The Forest seemed hushed, as if it was waiting for something to happen. As they passed the Keeper's cottage with its comforting glow of light, snow began to fall.

Charcoal loved snow. He chased the snowflakes as they fell and bit at the ground where they settled. He pounced on puddles to break the ice then lapped at the cold water as it oozed out of the cracks. Tess was laughing.

Suddenly, the certain knowledge that he was being watched made Charcoal stop. Tess looked up at the same time.

There on the other side of the bridge, stood the dapple grey mare. Her dark mane and tail made her look very beautiful in the snow. At her side was a coal-black foal, still wet from birth. On the foal's dark forehead was a perfect white star.

Charcoal waited while Tess knocked on the door of the Keeper's cottage. When she told the Keeper there was a foal, he looked at her as if she was mad. Everybody knows that ponies in the New Forest usually give birth in the spring. He put on his coat and boots.

"Long time since we've had a Christmas foal," he said, "Whereabouts did you see them?"

Tess and Charcoal led the Keeper back to the place where they had seen the mare and foal. They had vanished.

"Don't know about the little fella's chances in this weather" said the Keeper, "I'll call the Agister and have another look tomorrow."

That night when Tess and Charcoal went out into the garden to say goodnight to the stars, the sky was vast and clear. It was going to be a very cold night.

On Christmas Day, Tess and Charcoal returned to the same place. Theirs were the only footprints in the snow. There were no ponies there at all. They picked their way over the frozen heather and icy puddles to the other side of the moor.

All of a sudden, a fallow buck appeared on the path ahead of them. His coat gleamed white against the close-planted pine trees of the inclosure. The buck flicked his ears towards them. With a regal toss of his head, he turned and strode away into the trees.

"Do you think we should follow him?" Tess asked Charcoal, "In ancient times, if King Arthur saw a white buck he thought it was a sign that he should set off on a quest."

In response, Charcoal ran up to the gate and waited for her to open it. The buck paused for a moment then melted into the tangled paths that criss-crossed through the snow-covered hawthorn. Tess whispered to Charcoal to stay close and together they followed.

Within minutes, they had lost sight of him. Charcoal trotted on, sniffing the ground and letting the deer's strong scent guide him. Finally, his nose led them out of the thicket and they found themselves on a wide grassy track. Tess gasped. Charcoal stopped dead.

Not far ahead was a place where five tracks met to make the shape of a star. There in the centre stood the white buck, so still that it looked like one of Tess's sculptures.

The magical creature stared straight at Charcoal. For a moment he was locked in its gaze. Then in one bound it cleared a ditch and was gone.

It was only then that they saw the dapple grey mare.

"Oh look," Tess gasped, "it's our friend."

The tiny foal peered out from behind his mother's legs. The mare tried to push him back out of sight but he was too inquisitive. He took a few steps towards Tess and Charcoal.

"You're beautiful." said Tess.

The foal nodded his head and skipped back to his mother's side. This time, the owner's brand was just visible, buried deep in her winter coat.

On the way home, Tess called at the Keeper's cottage again.

"The foal seemed okay but the mare is getting a bit thin." she told him.

"Right" he said "I'll come and have a look."

But by the time they got back, the mare and foal had disappeared again.

"I think I saw a brand this time. It looked like a *T* and an *M*" said Tess.

"Can't think whose that would be," said the Keeper. "Not from round here anyway."

From then on, Charcoal's walks with Tess always seemed to lead them to the dapple grey mare and her black foal. One day they found them drinking at Fletcher's Water. Another day they were grazing in a clearing near Queen Bower. Despite the icy nights and a fresh fall of snow, the foal was growing stronger.

Each time Tess called at the Keeper's cottage to tell him where they'd seen them.

"Darned if I can find'un." he said. "You sure you're not seeing ghosts, Tess?"

Days turned into weeks and the foal was becoming more adventurous. None of the other mares had given birth to their foals yet. At this time of the year, the Forest ponies had only one thing on their minds and that was finding food.

"Poor little chap," said Tess, "You've nobody to play with, have you?"

Charcoal could see she was right. The little black foal kept trying to play with his mother but it just annoyed her.

Tess sat down on a fallen beech tree, studying the mare and foal in the way she often did. Charcoal took the chance to roll in the tough grass. He rolled and rolled until the itch on his back was scratched and his mind full of joy. He sat up, covered in crumbly brown leaves. He knew the foal had been watching him.

The grey mare whickered a warning but the foal took no notice. He stretched out his nose towards Charcoal and blew through his nostrils. Cautiously, Charcoal sniffed and licked the foal's muzzle. The foal drew back and curled his tongue over his soft pink nostrils as if to store the smell of his new friend. Charcoal stayed perfectly still, wondering what to do next.

The foal flicked his tail and snorted. Charcoal wagged his tail. The foal understood at once.

Charcoal pounced to one side and planted his front legs playfully. With a shrill whinny, the foal cantered around him with his tail held high. Charcoal pounced to the other side and the foal changed directions, circling him with glee.

From that day on, the foal would come trotting over as soon as he spotted Charcoal and Tess. His mother made it quite clear she didn't approve but she could do little to stop him.

The game always began in the same way. First they sniffed politely then the foal would skip sideways and suddenly they were playing. Sometimes they would play a kind of tag. Charcoal soon learnt to avoid the colt's heels, which he often kicked up when winning.

The other ponies pretended not to notice. They were hungry and slow with their own foals growing heavy inside them. Grateful for a break from the Christmas foal's pestering, they concentrated on searching for shoots of gorse and holly to eat.

Spring

January passed, then February and March. By the time the first curlew could be heard on the moor, Charcoal and the Christmas foal were best friends. Charcoal seemed to have a sixth sense for finding him but the Keeper never did.

Charcoal invented new games. He dived in and out of ditches and trees, playing hide and seek. Once he even found an old football in the bushes and persuaded the foal to push it along the grass with his nose.

The foal became less gangly and more agile. As he grew taller, he grew braver. He seldom worried how far he was from his mother. Bluebells turned the woods into a haze of blue mystery. Willow trees threw out showers of leaf buds in gold and green. From a hill far above the cottage, a cuckoo's rocking call drifted down on the breeze.

One morning, Tess and Charcoal woke up to see the first of the spring foals outside the window. It was a chestnut filly with legs so new that it hardly knew what to do with them.

Next day there was another: a beautiful bay colt with one white sock and a black mane and tail.

The following day there were two more foals. The day afterwards there were another three. After that it became impossible to count. Suddenly there were foals everywhere.

At Easter, sunshine brought visitors to the Forest in their hundreds. Cars jammed the roads. Caravan sites began to fill up. Car parks were surrounded by people with kites, balls and picnics.

Charcoal and Tess walked deeper and deeper into the Forest. The dapple grey mare and her Christmas foal retreated too.

"Hey" said the Keeper when he saw Tess one day in the village, "Think I might've seen that that foal of yours the other day."

"It isn't my foal," said Tess, but she sounded wistful.

That afternoon, she finished the kingfisher she had been carving and started whittling a large piece of yew into a mare and foal.

Summer

June was cool and wet. People from the camp sites huddled into the shops. Brave cyclists pedalled along the tracks wearing waterproofs. In the crowded tea rooms, the windows were steamy.

"Well if this is global warming, they can keep it," a man said to Tess outside the Post Office, "my feet are soaked."

Rainwater was overflowing in the gutters and streaming along the pavements. A small group of laughing children hung around on the footbridge, waiting for the next car to splash them in its wake or better still, to get stuck in the flooded ford.

In the Forest, everything grew green and lush. The mires stayed soggy and the streams full. Debris dams blocked the rivers and brought them on to flood.

As the days grew longer, the sun chased the rain clouds away. All the ponies of the New Forest were putting on much needed weight. The dapple grey mare was looking fit and well again. Her Christmas foal's summer coat was sleek and shiny. These days he was as eager to spend time eating as he was to play.

Often Charcoal would be satisfied with lying nearby in the shade while his friend munched grass with a steady, comforting *chomp, chomp* sound. He had plenty of other foals to play with now but he still greeted Charcoal as if he was the only person in the world he wanted to see.

September

Charcoal woke up with a start. Something was happening. Tess stirred in her sleep. Charcoal gave her a gentle nudge with his nose and whined softly. She opened her eyes.

"What is it Charkie?"

Charcoal whined again and barked.

"Okay, hang on." said Tess. She got up, yawning and pulled on a pair of jeans and a jumper.

At the end of the forest track where Tess and Charcoal lived, people were gathering with their trucks and trailers. Most of them were dressed warmly in country clothes. A few stood in the gaps between the lines of trees and other places where ponies might escape. Charcoal had seen all this before. It was the day of the drift.

Up on the hill, men and women riding fast ponies had already set off to start the round up. Tess took Charcoal back inside the gate at the end of the path to their cottage.

"We'll be safe here." she said.

It was a beautiful morning. Cobwebs glistened silver on the yellow gorse. Ponies grazed peacefully on the moor. For some of them, life was about to change forever but none of them knew that yet.

Charcoal sniffed the air, searching for a scent of his friend. In the distance he could hear the first sound of beating hooves. The ponies in front of the cottage stopped eating and raised their heads with their ears pricked. Charcoal felt Tess's hand gripping his collar.

"Hah, hah" came the shouts of the leaders as they sped over the rough grass with a band of mares and foals running ahead of them. Some of the ponies tried to head off through a gap in the alder and willow that lined the stream.

"Haarr, haarr" called the men and women posted to block their way. They raised their arms and shooed them back into the drift of galloping ponies.

Along they came, whinnying and galloping as fast as they could. Foals screamed for their mothers and mothers screamed for their foals and all the time the men and women were yelling "haar haar" which made them go all the faster until the track was a thunder of hooves and colours in ponies, ponies, ponies in every colour New Forest ponies can be: blacks, browns, bays, duns, creams, light greys, dark greys, roans, dapples and chestnuts.

Charcoal watched and watched with Tess hanging onto his collar as if it was the only thing to hang on to in the world. But they didn't see the dapple grey mare or her Christmas Foal.

When most of the ponies had been rounded up, a few riders went to bring in the stragglers. Tess waited with Charcoal until they too had trotted past with an air of triumph at being the last.

"Well Charkie, they weren't there, were they?" she said. She stroked Charcoal's head and went back into the cottage looking very thoughtful.

"But where are they?"

All that week, Tess and Charcoal looked for their friends but they weren't in any of their usual haunts. Even Charcoal's sixth sense failed him. There was no sight, no scent, no hint of the mare or foal in the air. Tess and Charcoal walked further and further but each day they returned home disappointed.

"If only that white buck would turn up again and lead us to them!" said Tess, but there was no sign of him either.

Charcoal pretended to be cheerful for Tess's sake but he was getting worried too. Tess spent more and more time working on the carving of the mare and foal.

"Well, perhaps they were rounded up after all." she said. "They might have been in another area."

*A*t Beaulieu Road, the sale yard was bustling with life. Men called to each other. Ponies jostled in the pens. Foals bunched together, still confused at being separated from their mothers. The auctioneer's voice sang out as if he was rapping a tune.

"Starting at ten, who'll give me fifteen? Nice little colt this. Fifteen, fifteen, who'll give me twenty? Nice little colt, don't lose him. Twenty, thank you, twenty five, thirty over there, forty, forty five, fifty...."

Charcoal jumped out of the old Land Rover that Tess had borrowed from a friend. He stood still as she attached his lead. They walked off towards the sale ring, leaving the Land Rover and pony trailer in the car park. Tess was up to something. Charcoal could feel her nervousness and a twinge of excitement by the way she was holding his lead.

Walking up and down between the pens, they saw what seemed like hundreds of foals. Each of them had a small circle of paper attached to its rump with a number on it. One or two were almost as black as the Christmas foal but none of them had the same white star on its forehead.

Tess held Charcoal's lead even tighter and pushed her way to the front of the crowd. From here they had a good view of the ring where the sales were taking place. Mingling with the familiar faces of the commoners, Charcoal saw a few people he didn't like the look of. A long low "grrrr" escaped from his throat before he could stop it.

"Hush Charcoal, not now!" hissed Tess. She stroked his back and he felt a bit easier.

A grey mare trotted into the sale ring alone. "Lovely little mare this, forest bred, good little mare, who'll start, who'll start at fifty?" chanted the auctioneer.

She was slightly dappled but her mane and tail were light. The man standing next to Tess and Charcoal raised his hand. A woman in the corner raised hers then several others did the same.

"Come on, nice little mare, one forty, chance of a new life, one fifty, one sixty in the corner." Finally the auctioneer tapped his hammer and pointed to the man next to Tess. "Sold!"

One pony after another came out of the holding pen into the ring. The steward shooed them around with his flag to show off their paces. Then it was the foals' turn. Some of them stood bewildered in the middle of the ring. Others cantered to and fro or bucked and spooked at the steward.

"Good little colt this, don't let him go. Unusual colour. I've got one hundred over there, who'll give me one ten? One hundred guineas, one ten, one twenty..."

Time after time, the auctioneer dropped his hammer and pointed to the person who had made the highest bid. Tess gripped the wooden rail so tight her knuckles were going white. She was clutching a piece of paper that meant she was allowed to bid.

"Fetching good money this year aren't they?" said a lady standing next to them.

"Yes." said Tess, "I'm not sure I'll be able to afford the one I've come for."

"Seen one you like then?" asked the lady.

"Yes but I'm not sure they're here."

"They?"

"Dapple grey mare with a black foal."

"Plenty of good foals this year." said the lady. "You'll find another."

"Not like this one." said Tess.

Charcoal leant up against her knee. She scratched the back of his ear in exactly the place where it was itchy. He licked her hand. The gate opened again and another foal came into the ring and stood blinking at the crowd. This wasn't the right one either.

At the end of the day, all the ponies and foals were either sold or loaded into lorries to be taken back by their owners.

"That's it then Charkie. Let's go home." said Tess.

As they were passing the corner of one of the pens, Charcoal caught a familiar scent. He wagged his tail at a tall man in a green coat and wellington boots. He was talking to another man, one that Charcoal didn't know.

"Afternoon," said the Agister. He had a nice smile in his voice, "Found any more stray ponies?"

"Actually I was wondering..." started Tess.

"Keeper thought you were seeing ghosts," said the Agister, "until I told him about the mare in the bog that night."

34

The man he'd been talking to laughed.

"I don't suppose you've seen the mare? I didn't see her rounded up in the drift and there's been no sign of her on the Forest since." said Tess.

"Can't say I have. Nice little lady she was. Dapple wasn't she?"

"That's right. The thing is she had a foal at Christmas time." said Tess. "Coal black he is, with a white star."

"Wait a minute!" said the other man, "Did you say the mare was a dapple grey? Did she have a much darker mane and tail?"

"That's right!"
Charcoal sensed Tess's excitement building.

"Sounds like old Tom Maddock's pony." said the man. He rubbed his beard.

"She did have a brand on her with a *T* and an *M* in it." said Tess.

"Yep. Tom Maddock. He only ran the one mare on the Forest."

"Where is he now?" asked Tess.

"Funny thing that. He reckoned she was sneaking in to see the black stallion at the stud near his place. Everybody thought he was making it up. Sure as eggs though, a dark foal always turned up around Christmas. Good Forest stock they were as well."

Charcoal's hairs were all standing on end and his tail was wagging. Every nerve in his body told him that Tess thought she had found the Christmas foal.

"Where can I find Tom Maddock?" she asked.

"St Nicholas' churchyard," said the man "he died last year - about September time."

"Oh no!"

"I believe his son has the place now. White Cottage they call it – over by Furzey Top. Thinking of selling it, I heard."

White Cottage was at the end of a long track that wound up a hill through a double line of gorse bushes. There was a red and green 'For Sale' board attached to the gatepost.

Tess parked the borrowed Land Rover outside. Charcoal rested his chin on the open window, watching as Tess knocked on the door. A young man wearing smart clothes opened it. He listened politely while Tess spoke.

"We haven't seen the pony since Dad died. I'd forgotten about her to be honest." said the young man. He looked at

Tess as if he was trying to make up his mind about something.

"I tell you what," he said, "Dad wouldn't have wanted her to go to the sales. If you can find her, you can have her."

"Really? Are you sure?"

"We've more than enough to do here, what with selling the house and everything. I need to get back to London. The last thing I want is a pony!"

"It 's a couple of days since we've seen her." said Tess.

"Here's my address. Write if you find her and I'll sign something to say she's yours."

"There's a foal as well," said Tess, her voice was trembling, "a colt."

"Oh dear," said Tom Maddock's son, "Is there any chance you could take him too?"

When Tess jumped back into the car, the air buzzed with happiness. She drove off singing at the top of her voice.

"Right!" said Tess to Charcoal as soon as they were home, "Let's go and find them."

Charcoal was more than ready. He had no idea why but he had a strong feeling that there was no time to lose. He ran ahead, carrying his tail like a banner.

By the time dusk came, Tess was exhausted and Charcoal was confused. Several times he thought he had picked up the right scent but each time he lost it. They couldn't find the dapple grey mare or her Christmas foal anywhere.

"Perhaps it's just as well, Charkie. I don't even know where we'd have kept him." As she spoke, she was whittling away thoughtfully at the carving of the mare and foal.

There was a loud knock on the back door. Tess jumped. Charcoal barked once and ran to the door. Tess opened it.

"Evening Tess!" It was Kate from next door. "I was hoping to find you in." She made a fuss of Charcoal, rubbing his ears and scratching his back.

"Is everything okay?" asked Tess.

"Well, it's my niece's birthday next week and I've left it a bit late to find a special present. Then I had this brainwave. I'd like to buy one of your sculptures."

In the living room, Tess picked out the kingfisher carving and held it up. Kate didn't even look at it. She was staring at the carving of the mare and foal.

"That's the one! It's going to be wonderful." she said "How much will you be asking for it?"

Tess went white. She stroked the little wooden foal's nose with her finger.

"I'm sorry," she said, "I can't sell this one."

That night, Tess stayed up for ages finishing the carving. Charcoal flopped onto his bed as soon as he'd eaten his dinner. His paws twitched and his nostrils quivered as he ran through his dreams, following the mysterious white buck.

*N*ext morning, Charcoal took charge as soon as they left the cottage.

"Where are you off to, Charkie?" said Tess but she followed him, struggling to keep up. At Highland Water, he ran upstream until they reached a shallow place where Tess could cross.

They scrambled over fallen trees and waded through boggy patches to a place they had never been before. Even so, Charcoal knew it straight away. It was the place the white buck had shown him in his dream. He stopped at a gate, his tail taut and his nose stretched out. Tess opened the latch and the gate swung open.

Here another stream cut deep into wet grassland. Birch trees swayed like silver wands. A grey heron stood on one leg in the flood water. A small band of fallow deer were tiptoeing along the edge. It was so quiet.

Then Charcoal heard something shuffling in the trees. The deer heard it too. The heron threw an accusing look at Tess then rose up and away on wide grey wings.

In a flicker of light, a pony emerged, slowly and painfully.

She was a light dapple grey with a dark mane and tail. Charcoal recognised her immediately but he didn't go bounding over. Instead he lay down quietly with one front paw crossed over the other. The mare was desperately lame. She could hardly walk.

Tess walked towards her, talking in a whisper:

"Hey little lady. Where have you been?" She reached out and stroked the mare's neck. She ran her fingers gently over the *T* and the *M* branded just behind her withers.

"Tom Maddock's pony." whispered Tess. The mare flicked her ears but her eyes were dim.

"Where's your foal?"

The mare let out a deep breath like a sigh. She allowed Tess to stroke her muzzle. There was an enormous gash down her front leg. It was horribly swollen and the wound was covered with dried blood and flies.

Tess pulled her mobile phone out of her pocket. This time she rang the number marked 'Vet'.

Almost an hour had passed before the vet arrived. By now the mare was down, lying on her side. Tess had offered her anything in her pack that a pony might possibly want to eat but she didn't want anything.

"Oh god" said the vet, "she must have been hit by a car – a few days ago by the look of things. I don't know how she's kept going."

He ran his hand down the mare's leg. She flinched but didn't try to get up.

"The car must have been going at a hell of a speed," said the vet, "my guess is that the driver didn't even stop, let alone report hitting her."

"Is there anything you can do?" asked Tess.

"The kindest thing would be to put her to sleep."

Tears ran down Tess's face as she held the dapple grey mare's head.

"Does she have a name?" asked the vet.

"I was going to call her Ghost" said Tess.

The vet smiled and stroked the pony's face.
"Goodbye brave Ghost." he said.

After the vet had left and the mare's body had been taken away, Tess sat on the wet grass for a long time, stroking Charcoal's head. The heron returned. A tawny owl flew out of the wood, across the clearing and into a copse. The water shone like crystal in the sun. A roe deer sauntered over to take a long, slow drink. It was as if she and Charcoal were invisible.

What had happened to her foal? Had he been hit too? He was so dark he would be difficult to see on the road at night. Neither of them had been wearing a reflective collar as many of the ponies did.

Charcoal jumped up and licked Tess's face. He licked and licked until she started to laugh.

"What are you doing? " she said.

He let out a loud "woof" that echoed through the forest and woke the heron from his trance. The roe deer disappeared in one leap. A squirrel chattered angrily from the fence. Rabbits scattered.

Tess pulled herself up onto her feet, stiff from sitting on the damp grass and aching with sadness.

"Come on Charkie, let's go home" she said.

Charcoal had other ideas. In his dream, the white buck had shown him a lot more than this. His tail was high again as he scampered off into the wood, willing Tess to follow.

Tess hurried after him through a small wood of ancient oak, knotted holly and towering beech trees. Soon they were on open ground and climbing a small hill. The top was crowned in gorse. Beyond the gorse Charcoal found a gravel track that led to a white cottage.

"It's Tom Maddock's place!" said Tess. "Poor, brave Ghost must have been trying to come home."

The sign on the board outside had been changed. It now read 'SOLD'. There were no curtains in the windows and the cottage was empty. Charcoal ignored all that and ran around the back. Puffing a bit from the hill, Tess followed more slowly.

The paddock gate was open and ragwort had been allowed to grow tall and yellow.

"I bet Tom Maddock wouldn't have liked that," said Tess.

Charcoal let out a high-pitched "Woof!" more like an excitable puppy than a full grown dog. There was a scuffling noise then a shrill, familiar whinny from the ramshackle shelter in the corner. Out came a handsome young foal with a deep black coat and a white star on his forehead.

"We've found you!" said Tess.

But the foal stared straight past Tess and Charcoal as if he was expecting to see somebody else.

"I'm sorry." said Tess. "She's gone." She ran her hand over the foal's back and legs. There was a small cut on his face and a few nicks on one of his knees.

"Looks more like a fight with some brambles than an accident with a car." she said, sounding very relieved. "Now all we've got to do is find somewhere to keep you."

Then she had an idea.

*C*harcoal watched as Tess and Kate unbolted the trailer and lowered the ramp. The foal scrambled down onto the soft grass. Blinking, he looked around and seemed to like what he saw. He started eating immediately.

"I've asked the vet to come just to check him over properly." said Tess.

"I still don't see why you needed my paddock." said Kate, "Your cottage has forest rights doesn't it?"

"Yes but only mares can roam on the forest all year round," explained Tess, "he's a colt and he'll soon be a stallion."

"Well it works well enough for me." said Kate, "I'm more than happy for you to use the paddock in return for your wonderful sculpture of the mare and foal. I'll let you into a secret though, I'm going to keep it for myself and find something else for my niece!"

Tess laughed.

By the time the vet arrived, the foal had persuaded Charcoal to play. Tess had a job catching him for the vet to do his examination.

"Nothing much wrong with this one that some loving care won't put right" he said, "What are you going to call him?"

"I've only ever called him *little foal*!" said Tess.

"He'll need a grander name than that if he is going to sire some foals of his own one day."

The foal strolled up to Tess and nudged her arm, nibbling her jacket. The star on his forehead gleamed white on his beautiful dark face.

"I'll call him *Seren*," she said, pulling his ear gently, "it means star."

Seren snorted and cantered over to where Charcoal was snoozing in the sun. Charcoal woke up and licked the foal's nose.

"Well, you don't often see that!" said the vet. "They really are the best of friends aren't they?"

Charcoal felt someone watching. He glanced over to the other side of the paddock. For a moment he thought he saw an old man standing in the shade of the yew tree with his arm tucked around a dapple grey mare. He yawned and stretched. They were only ghosts.

Charcoal has his own pages on our website!

There's loads more to learn about Charcoal's world
and you can find out about future books in the series
if you **visit him on**
www.greendragonpublishing.co.uk

...and a note from the author

You've probably guessed how much I love living in the New Forest. For me, seeing ponies roam freely is part of its special magic.

Although the story you've just read isn't actually true, road accidents involving the animals of the New Forest are all too real. Just as I was finishing this book, a mare was hit by a speeding car at the end of the road where I live.

This is why Jo and I decided to donate 10% of any profit we make from this edition of *Charcoal and the Christmas Foal* to the Verderers of the New Forest to help them buy reflective collars for the ponies and work to reduce the number of accidents.

Also

Please remember that Charcoal is a very unusual dog. There aren't many dogs that can be trusted near ponies, other livestock, wild animals or their young.

Whatever you do don't let your own dog try to play with the foals or go too close to any of the animals! If you see deer close by, it is always best to put your dog on the lead.

Most of all, I hope you will have great fun in the New Forest and love it as much as I do.

Mel Newman